THE CONQUEROR

GARMADON'S ACTIVITY JOURNAL

It's awesome, isn't it?

This book has been designed, written and drawn by a warrior who's never been defeated; a mighty conqueror seeking vengeance on the ninja; a great father, husband and brother ...
in other words, by an extremely accomplished warlord – ME – THE GREAT, PROUD GARMADON!

BEFORE WE START, IF YOU WANT TO HELP CREATE THIS BOOK WITH ME, YOU MUST FILL IN AND SIGN THE FOLLOWING STATEMENT:

I, ...,
aged .... am .... metres tall and do solemnly declare, that I will never, EVER, reveal any secrets of the bravest, smartest, most powerful, undefeated master of martial arts and the soon-to-be ultimate ruler of Ninjago Island and its surroundings — GARMADON!

Place and date: ....
Signature: ....

It's me, your favourite warlord!
Coming back to conquer all!

Don't you dare stick your photo here!
This page is for my picture.

Hmm ... OK, I see it means a lot to you ... you can have it.
I'll put mine on the next page.

Time flies, things change. Here's me, when I was much younger ...

LOOK AT MY HAIR!
I CAN'T BELIEVE I LIKED IT ...
WASN'T I HANDSOME, THOUGH?
A PERFECT FUTURE RULER!

But enough talking! Turn the page and let's get started.

Before we go ANY further, I must know more about you. Fill in the answers to these questions:

Who would you never want to fight?

....

Who do you trust the most?

....

Who would you tell everything to?

....

Who is your hero?

....

Who would you like to have as your neighbour?

....

Who is the most powerful of them all?

....

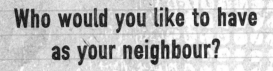

IF 'GARMADON' APPEARS IN THE MAJORITY OF YOUR ANSWERS THEN I WILL ALLOW YOU TO HELP ME CONQUER NINJAGO CITY!

LET ME TELL YOU A LITTLE ABOUT MYSELF.

I have room in my life for exactly one thing: conquering.

I love conquering!

I love conquering buildings, cars, shops, parks, streets and all the bricks in Ninjago City!

Garmadon loves conquering

Garmadon loves conquering

I love conquering everything in Ninjago City!

GO AHEAD AND WRITE ABOUT OTHER THINGS I LOVE CONQUERING. IT WON'T BE DIFFICULT BECAUSE I LOVE CONQUERING EVERYTHING!

Garmadon loves conquering

Garmadon loves conquering

Draw me as the ruler of Ninjago City here!

And now it's going to become reality! I'm going to write down how I plan to conquer Ninjago City, step by step! Or brick by brick ...

TODAY I WAS JUST SITTING THERE, NURTURING MY NEGATIVE EMOTIONS, WHEN I DECIDED THAT I NEEDED A GREAT WEAPON TO TAKE OVER NINJAGO CITY!

BUT WHAT COULD IT BE?

A gigantic iron ball that could roll right through Ninjago City! (But what would I reign over then?)

Dark robots, that could defeat the defenders of Ninjago City! (But what if they want to be rulers, too?)

A ray from outer space that would transform the inhabitants of Ninjago Island into my dancing servants. (But where could I get the ray from?)

... I had my team!
These brave I.T. nerds will design and build lots
of massive, scary battle machines for me!
I'LL USE THEM TO HELP ME CONQUER
THE WORLD OF NINJAGO!

My thoughts on evil conquering machines

Any machine designed for conquering Ninjago City needs to:

1. Look awesome!

2. Be at least five times bigger than an average warrior

3. Instil fear and horror in everyone

4. Spread chaos

5. Destruction

6. Be something other than a small crocodile ...

7. ... or a little shark

8. Have fangs, claws, stingers and all those pointy things

9. And have a scary name

Now YOU write something, because I'm out of ideas.

10

11

12

13

14

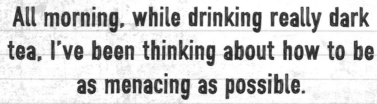

All morning, while drinking really dark tea, I've been thinking about how to be as menacing as possible.

I've always thought dangerous sea creatures are really menacing, so that's the theme I'm using ...

... for my Shark Army!

Design scary armour for them here. After that, things will start to get really evil.

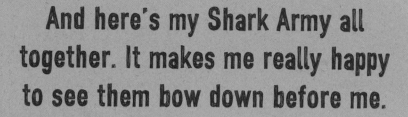

And here's my Shark Army all together. It makes me really happy to see them bow down before me.

Label the pieces to complete the plans of my combat vehicles. Then, colour them in.

They need to be built from bricks and I need as many of them as there are fish in the sea! As you can see, I have all the bricks I need to conquer Ninjago City! I can already see my vehicles tearing into the city like a sea storm ...

Now I need to stop writing so I can complete my work and finally become the ruler of Ninjago City.

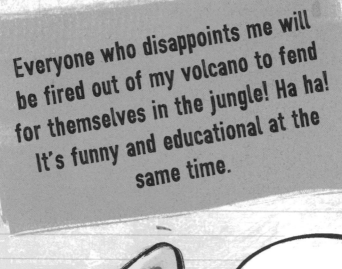

Everyone who disappoints me will be fired out of my volcano to fend for themselves in the jungle! Ha ha! It's funny and educational at the same time.

REMEMBER, YOU'D BETTER NOT DISAPPOINT ME EITHER!

FLYING OUT ON FORCED HOLIDAY!
Draw a few more of my disappointments getting a free-flying lesson from me.

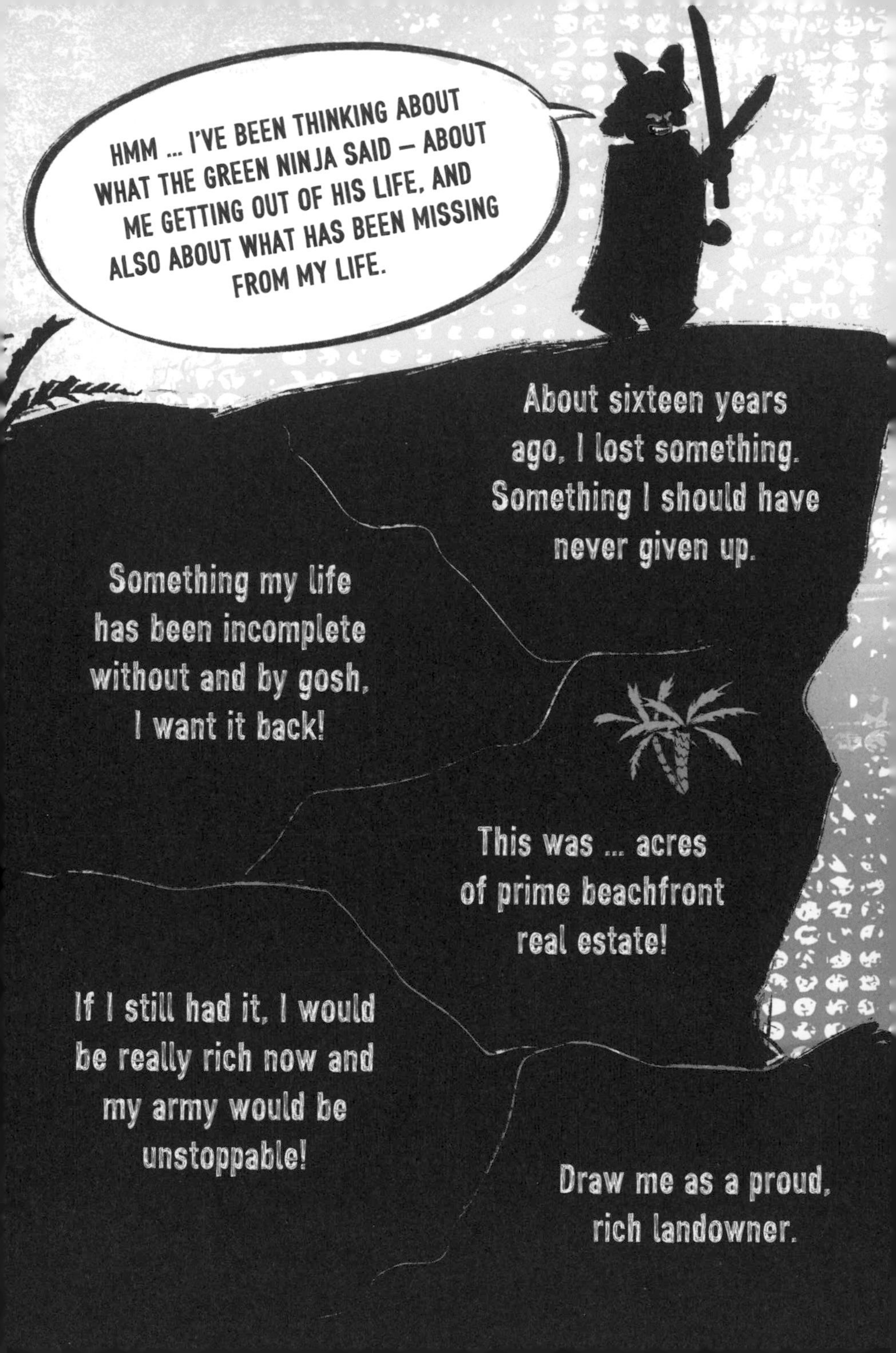
HMM ... I'VE BEEN THINKING ABOUT WHAT THE GREEN NINJA SAID – ABOUT ME GETTING OUT OF HIS LIFE, AND ALSO ABOUT WHAT HAS BEEN MISSING FROM MY LIFE.
About sixteen years ago, I lost something. Something I should have never given up.
Something my life has been incomplete without and by gosh, I want it back!
This was ... acres of prime beachfront real estate!
If I still had it, I would be really rich now and my army would be unstoppable!
Draw me as a proud, rich landowner.

I SHOULD BE STANDING ON THE SHORE IN FRONT OF A ROW OF GRAND MANSIONS.

Wearing my Ninjago City ruler's crown too, of course.

Give the finishing touches to my new mech by colouring it in!

My first orders as the ruler of Ninjago City:

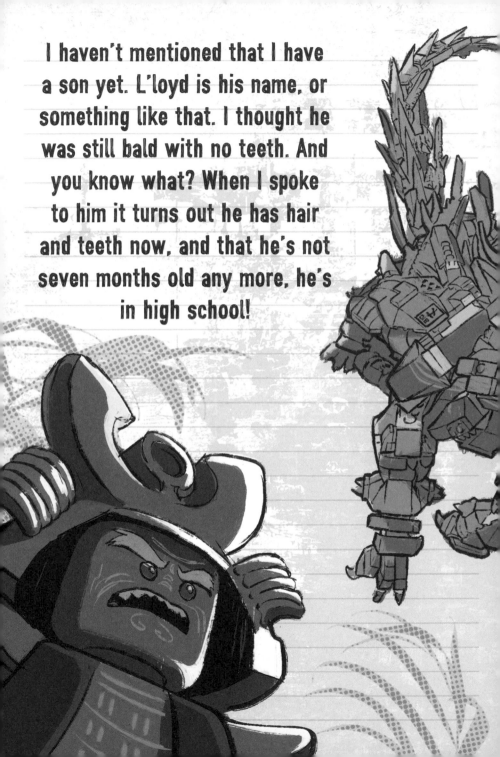

I haven't mentioned that I have a son yet. L'loyd is his name, or something like that. I thought he was still bald with no teeth. And you know what? When I spoke to him it turns out he has hair and teeth now, and that he's not seven months old any more, he's in high school!

I couldn't talk to him for long because I had to continue planning how to fix the Green Ninja problem!

FACE IT, GARMADON! WE ARE UNSTOPPABLE!

If I only knew where he was hiding ...

I need to think of a way to catch him ...

I know! Maybe I'll build a giant dragon-catching mech from which I'll shoot out a very big net.

Or I'll lure the Green Ninja into an enormous, very sticky mud trap.

AND NOW IT'S YOUR TURN. SHOW ME
WHAT YOU'VE GOT, MINION! WHERE
DO YOU THINK THE GREEN NINJA
COULD BE HIDING?

How to spot a ninja

(Draw a ninja – but don't make him too attractive!)

head full of ideas

silly mask
(making identification
more difficult)

weapons
(I'd rather they
didn't have any)

Finish the description of the ninja warrior to help me out.

Make me happy by destroying the pictures of the ninja!

Draw some ridiculous skis for the green one.

Give the white one red clothes and a SANTA HAT.

The red one will look good with BIG SUNGLASSES and a LARGE MOUSTACHE. HE HE HE

Behold the wall of shame!
These are the nasty ninja
who constantly defy me.
You should definitely
doodle over them ...

HOW will you change
the rest?

Speaking of ninja ... I've been dreaming about an
enormous, massive duel with my greatest enemy!
Maybe with the Green Ninja? Or maybe with my brother,
Master Wu? (Have I mentioned that I have a brother?)
Hmm ... the duel would take place in dramatic weather.
During a thunderstorm! A hurricane!
Rain, snow, flooding and an earthquake!
(OK, maybe I'm exaggerating ... a thunderstorm will do.)

Choose an opponent for me, then finish the comic to show the results of the greatest duel of all time.

You might want to add stickers, too!

THE REAL STORY OF THE NINJAGO CITY CONQUEST

Turbulent waters were lashing against the shores of Ninjago City. Suddenly, the waves whirled around and a giant figure emerged from the raging sea foam. It was an enormous mech, controlled by the future ruler of Ninjago City, and it was heading towards the shore! The eagle-eyed conqueror contemplated his future kingdom. He wondered what those ninja would do when they saw his new mech. They'd probably be scared and run away! Just then, lots of Shark Army vehicles appeared. Their chief signalled for them to attack! The conquest of Ninjago City was ON!

Wow, you're never gonna believe this! The Green Ninja is L'loyd!!!

He's just taken off his mask and shown his face to me ...

Why didn't anyone tell me?

So, I need to finish this book right now because I have to snatch that Ultimate Weapon from him.

And he wanted to use the Ultimate Weapon on me.

Son or not ... I need to win this one!

And let me tell you one thing ...

I SHALL RETURN WITH A REALLY WICKED PLAN! MWAH, HA, HA!

ABOUT THE AUTHORS

GARMADON

Garmadon is everyone's favourite warlord and greatest leader! (The greatest ever in fact, although even that doesn't give him enough credit.) His battles will always be remembered and children will learn about him at school. He's always full of darkness — incredibly able, brilliant and merciless to enemies. He is highly intelligent, a genius military strategist and a master of martial arts. Put simply, he's an undefeated warrior and mighty conqueror seeking vengeance on the ninja.

NOW IT'S YOUR TURN. WRITE SOMETHING ABOUT YOURSELF AND HOW MUCH YOU WORSHIP ME HERE:

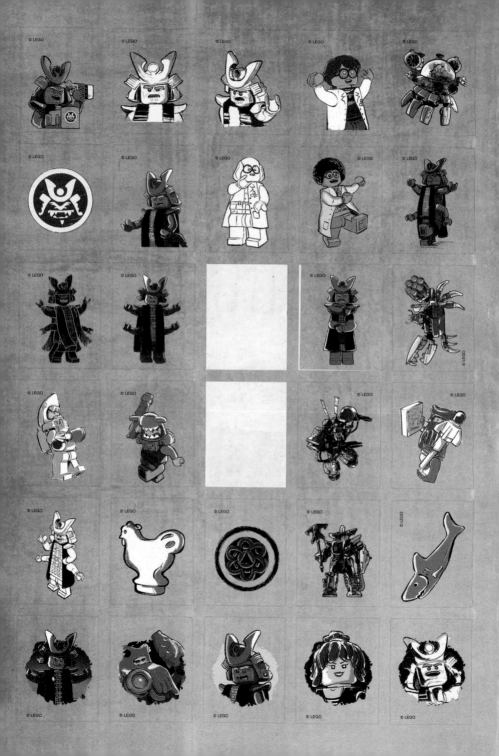